WILD OATS AND FIREWEED

Books by Ursula K. Le Guin

WILD OATS AND FIREWEED

URSULA K. LeGUIN

NEW POEMS

Harper & Row, Publishers, New York
Cambridge, Philadelphia, San Francisco, Washington
London, Mexico City, São Paulo, Singapore, Sydney

Copyright acknowledgments appear on page 89.

FIRST EDITION

Designer: Sidney Feinberg

Library of Congress Cataloging-in-Publication Data

Le Guin, Ursula K., date
 Wild oats and fireweed.

 I. Title.

PS3562.E42W55 1987	811'.54	87-45222
ISBN 0-06-055101-1		88 89 90 91 92 MPC 10 9 8 7 6 5 4 3 2 1
ISBN 0-06-096227-5 (pbk.)		88 89 90 91 92 MPC 10 9 8 7 6 5 4 3 2 1

Contents

"Child on Forest Road" by Wynn Bullock

Where's the little one going
alone on the oak-forest road?
What does the child hear?

Maybe she's going to meet
the woman coming from there.

She's old, she's old,
her feet are bare,
her hair uncombed.
Far in the forest
and sweet she whistles,
"I'm coming, little one, little one,
coming on home."

Her feet are bare,
her hair uncombed,
the child who stops and listens, listens,
all by herself on the oak-forest road.

PART ONE: PLACES

Northern B.C.

Land forms
the mind.
Ideas fill these bogs,
low hills, long leas
by glaciers formed.
Hands
farmed,
cut, dug, deformed
some lands.
Not these.
Land informs
mind as water
the hills in working to the sea.

Flight 65 to Portland

For Jane

Innumerable delicate rectangles
greyblack streaked
white diagonally scratched
scraped across corner
/exact/ to corner by the North
West mathematic Cold
wind over the flat vast
(totally maternal) Dakotas

Three Ohio Poems

1. ROBINSONS' FARM

South is a black cat and a white barn.
North a high hill in cornstalks.
West a round window full of wind.
East through a screen
of trees finely dividing
a far air, rising
over Ohio all the moon.

2. SPRING, ROBINSONS' FARM

If you leave me long enough alone
it will just come talking its way out
like the creek today
I found below bare trees
coming out from under
a rock talking easily and quietly
and clearly over stones and leaves
and shining and going not in any hurry
but to the sea where else?
Like that just leave me
alone and I will be welling.

3. IN THAT OHIO

For Sheila Jordan

They ring bells in the marshes,
little bells in the evening in choruses.
It is trilling season.
A bird before sunrise
sings B, B-flat, B, over and over
and all day these three notes
are just out of hearing. Violets
flaunt, springs start from dirt
as if there was nothing to flowing.
Mists loom along the Kokosing,
clouds bank colors, wind irises
vastly, vanishes suddenly, rain
widens and ceases: a weather
immoderate, generous, central.
That Ohio, late March to early April,
full moon to no moon,
was a long way from edges,
the salt harshness, the bitter ends;
a lap, a bowl, an offering, allowing
two hawks above a field
at play, layering spirals
one over the other higher and higher,
to prove the breadth of continent, the depth of air,
and the dimension of their constancy.

NM

The cloud people are women
long-necked, long-striding,
a round jar balanced
high on the head.

Shadows of the white,
    the grey, the black jars,
inscribed with spirals,
    terraces, lightning,
pass over the plains

from mountain to mountain
in silence, as the tall
women return bearing water
from the old, deep well.

Five South, One North

i
This is what happens in the Great
Valley of California:
wind moves in the grasses
grasses move in the wind

ii
The lives of jackrabbits killed by cars
on American highways
hammer like hail on the doors of compassion

iii
From a part of California
on a high-fog morning
where the bare hills
rise interfolded one beyond another
going up ever remoter
and fainter and more golden
I learned how to get to glory

iv
Lark goes up singing singing
but comes down silent silent
so nobody can follow
her to the little round warmths
in the grasses grasses grasses

Crazy Knobby Beauty and Smooth

TWO BEACH POEMS

For Alice and John

i

In this garden of great pleasure
some of the people live already.
I have made others come here
until the wind moves them
or sand or water covers them.
They are all end-products of delight
of the eternal machineries,
and each one took eons:
the sea-urchin shell, the broken abalone,
the striped stone and the cross-striped stone,
the holey stone, the two two-eyed sandstones,
the split wood and the divided reed,
the twisted tube of copper,
the sea-worn branch with its eccentric curve.
All are living together in the great pleasure
that I feel for them in the sunlight
between fogs fifteen feet from the breakers
of the Straits of Juan de Fuca
on the sand between two driftlogs
in an interim of countable hours.
The five stars of the Swan
or the places the wind comes from
or my eyes and knees
or a few sandgrains
on the beach of any ocean
are the corners of the garden of great pleasure.

ii

Unaccountable!
The noblest is humble.
The most beautiful crouches
before the lump of sandstone.
The smooth-skinned warm rosy
quartz that sings the fingers
a wonderful geology, this curving maiden
came downstream from the snow
before mad Columbus, maybe
before canoes; she knows
enough; so she curves over,
blessing the ephemeral
in the armless gesture
of the sea-borne, the foam-mother.

Luwit

She dances,
she dances,
the lady dances.
Ashes, ashes, all fall down!
Shakti, Shakti,
blew your stack,
your virgin crown
is boiling mud,
forestfire, earthshake,
gas, ash, filth, flood,
your breath death. You are
a darkness on the western wind,
a curtain falling for a thousand miles.
O lady you've blown it,
you're grit between our teeth,
motes in our eyes,
rose-salmon sunsets clear to Reykjavik.
Your face is dirty, seamed, burnt, scarred.
You killed the old man and his cats,
ten billion tiny fish,
and broke the lake your mirror.
Bad luck lady.
The grey Quaker woke
and the cities of the plain
beheld, and shook,

cast ashes on their heads,
crying Lady be good!
Unkind: O plumed
unmaker,
fire-womb,
O dancer!

(4 June 1980)

Prologue: Concerning Violence

The earth fell on the earth. It looked like cloud
but it was dirt: the planet turning on itself.

Rock, slag, dust, earthgas, earthfire, earthwork.

A column of boiling stone. Ponderous.

From a distance thunderblue, but in itself earthdark,
grey, brown, black: a mountain inside out.

And the lightning struck, and struck, and struck.
Dancing like a hopjack strung up on the groundcloud,
the stoneplume, jagging between earth and earth,
the lightning struck, and struck, and struck.

The forest was dead in the first five minutes.

At Meta Lake*

There are no mirrors here.

This is a labyrinth where none of the ways
        leads in or out
but all the arrows point the same direction.

---

*Meta Lake is on Mt. St. Helens in the blast zone, where the trees were not vaporized, but blown down. It was found in 1980 that some fish in the little lake had actually survived the eruption and the pollution of the water by dead vegetation, ashfall, bacterial blooms, etc. The fish did not, however, survive the United States Department of Fish and Game, who removed them from the lake to identify and count them.

21

It is easy to compare to Hell,
but then where are you?
Hell has to do with justice.
This has not.
This has nothing to do with us at all
        except as we are fir, are fern,
        are trout, are jay, are elk.
The bones of deer are in this ash.
This is not punishment.
We have no claim on it. It does not regard us.
Our crimes can only imitate.
It is we who hold the mirror up.
This is not Hell.

But is it wrong to say the names of hope?
The names break through the grey crust,
        tough, sweet, and seedy:
        fireweed,
        pearly everlasting,
        vetch.
    Some grass. Some bracken fern.
    A brownish-orange mushroom the size of a thumbtack
        down in a hollow of the huge dead trees
        by the stinking shores
        of the little, sick, dark lake.
(Imagine!
        morning sunlight filtering through leaves
        to the clear water, and the birds waking!)

Yet there are wings:
        migrants,
        a sudden quickness in the dull air,
        gone.
And the seeds, the spores, break through.

The germ is powerful.
Thumb-high seedlings under blue shadow of May snow,
ignorant when the black blast came:
now they stand one here
one there,
small green prayersticks,
feathers, powers,
in this steep dust encumbered with the dead.

The Car

The car sits
tiny
and most terrible.

The beercans in the back
imploded.

The car sits
glassless, rusting,
flattened out a bit.

Authority has put a chainlink fence around it
to keep out looters
or to hold the horror in.

The car sits
where they parked it
when they went up to their mine
under the big dark trees, in ferns and huckleberry,
        the thrushes singing, maybe,
            sunlight in the needles of the firs.
As I went walking one morning so early,

As I went walking one morning of May
        it was a long day
        longer than any other day
        a labyrinth
        from dark to way into the dark
        by way of dust
        by way of fire
        by way of ash
        by way of rain.
          A maze
of the bones of children
and the bones of deer.

To Walk In Here

To walk in here is to stop pretending.

What's real? Grey dust,
        a dead forest.
Entropy moves quickly to its end.
O desolation!
        What's real?
        says the fireweed lightly casting
        its words upon the wind.

To walk in here is to stop pretending
that what we do matters
all that much. Less in the long run
than the fireweed: to the others.

To ourselves we matter
terribly.

That there will be summer
ever
is the responsibility of others
more careful than ourselves.

They do not look us in the face.

> The gulfs of air
> are full of blowing rain,
> between us and the crater,

> the small, cold rain of autumn.

(October 1981)

III. Back in the Red Zone

It is not a place
but a condition of being
as different from life
as death, yet
bridgelike: abrupt
end beginning.
Wet green to skeleton grey
in one moment that day
and still now:
utter
difference.
A word in a foreign language,
but recognised
with tears.

Hiroshima, Nagasaki,
Dresden, the London docks,
they had no beauty but the fireweed.
They were places.
This is not. No longer,
or not yet. It is beautiful.
It is changing being.

Spirit Lake that was,
Soul Lake now, maybe.
Desolate, sickening,
choked up, being pumped out
by big machines like in a modern hospital,
engines sucking excess away,
attentive intercoms and telephones,
trucks and cars anting in and out
with portable toilets for the men,

all men of course, the doctors
working hard, long hours
under the steaming toadstool in the hollow tooth
miles across and above them,
uttering
difference, but not listened to.
Where is away?
We are a busy little species.
How we rush about!
Dirt roads all directions in the ash
and loggers on the two-way radio:
>I need some tielines here
>how's Jack OK
>two-thirty-five
>there's oil spraying everywhere
>aawheeeee
>hang on what sizes line was that
>where are you now
>OK   OK
and as in the vast and cold blue hollow
the plume turns faint, the crater's edge faint rose,
>goodnight
>see you tomorrow, hey
>OK
and silence.
Silence and moonlight on the lake!
the terrible thick sick silted poison lake
self-dammed: making changes.
Soul Lake, working itself free.
Things have to die, Jack.
You have to let them die.

This bright morning after,
back to life, to the September forests,

the sweet winds, the windows of my house,
from that place no place
I have come with a word I cannot speak.
I have come back down the mountain.
I have crossed the bridge
across the lake.
There is no bridge across the lake.
Look, look, the bright plume shining!

(September 1983)

PART TWO: WOMAN

Pane

You have painted (out) me
consenting
as a silver film
molecularly thin
backed by a slick
of black.
Where am I? Look
and you'll see yourself
                    clearly,
(and the backwords,
unspeakable)
comforting in
Silence.
Nowhere
my being: (a) reflecting
(of) your seeming (or) appearing
so that you can
believe in yourself being
                    clearly.
O But If I should Not consent
        and scratch
                flake off
                        get dim
                                transparent,
the black peeling
to bare the silver
to tarnish and vanish,
what would be left
but a glass
        clearly

and you if you (dare)
look in it seeing
what you have not seen:

What is the glass
between?

The Maenads

Somewhere I read
that when they finally staggered off the mountain
into some strange town, past drunk,
hoarse, half-naked, blear-eyed,
blood dried under broken nails
and across young thighs,
but still jeering and joking, still trying
to dance, lurching and yelling, but falling
dead asleep by the market stalls,
sprawled helpless, flat out, then
middle-aged women,
respectable housewives,
would come and stand nightlong in the agora
silent
together
as ewes and cows in the night fields,
guarding, watching them
as their mothers
watched over them.
And no man
dared
that fierce decorum.

Apples

Judeochristian men should
not be allowed
to eat apples, they
have been bellyaching
for millennia
that my mother made
them eat an apple
that gave them a bellyache.
From now on only women
eat apples. Also
nonjudeochristian men
if they can do it
without whining. Also
children if their mother
says so or if they can
steal them and
get away with it.

And if a woman wants
she is to wear snakes
for bracelets
and her hair
is to hiss at any man
who cannot resist her
and strike him so he falls
stone stiff and gets stuck
into a glass coffin
like a bank
and nobody will come to kiss him.
But the snakes

coiling down from round arms
across the baby's head
and the milky nipples,
will be fed
with apples.

To Saint George

Woman is worm.
Toothless and trodden-on
earthworm, leaven of garden.
She knows the tongueworm
and bigbrother cockworm
and heartworm. She knows
the wombworm
nestling within her.
She knows beginnings
and undersides. She knows
the oneworm, the roundworm
unending, hollow, all, egg,
being the dragon.
Saint, better get her
before she talks.

Of Course She Is Frigid

Frigid yes
beyond your six-inch thermometer
a mile deep
I lie along high valleys
imponderably massive
and luminously cold
bearing very slowly down
from the immense and central source
and place and uttermost of ice
over your cities of little sticks
to reform the land.
I leave great lakes
and empty plains behind me.
In what age will I reach
that south that warmth
where I can quicken and run free
slipping through the fingers of children?

For Virginia Kidd

The patience of women
is stupid and beautiful as the patience of donkeys.

The impatience of men
is stupid and terrible as the impatience of horses.

The impatience of women
is like thunderstorms among mountains.

The patience of men
is like streams in the valleys.

Dos Poesias Para Mi Diana

I came back to the island. I rented a little and precarious cabin, not far
from the place where I lived for six years. The house seems to be at point
of falling at any moment. But will not do it. I will keep to stay her there,
on the water-land. I love the place, in the border of the forest, poplars
and palms surrounding, and so many birds crossing the space. . . . I bring
the child in my ear.

Diana's letter of 10 September 1984

THE TWINS

Tiny dreamchildren,
soulchildren,
silver and turquoise,
very old children.

One in your ear like a whisper
under the tawny hair,
by the river in the shadow of palms
and shadow of poplars.

One in the prow of a toy canoe,
a soulboat of the Yurok,
with four stones from the world's corners,
and one from the middle.

Listen to the river
that whispers to your cabin!
It is the sweet cold Klamath
flashing with salmon, under the redwoods.
North, north, the child is calling.

And the redwood boat
carries its passenger rocking
past my sleep on the deep waters
of the Paraná. . . .
South, south, the child is calling.

THE DREAM

I am in the dream of the puma,
in the night of the huntress,
the darkness the color of gold.

I have lost my way and wander
in terror beside the bloodstreams
in the shadows between rivers.

All ways are the right way
in the dream of the puma, the pampas,
the forests, the flowers, the freedoms,
the darkness the color of gold.

Amtrak Portland to Seattle

"For a tear is an intellectual thing"

I'd like to cry
and the woman across the aisle
is crying
in silence.
Conductor threatens running kids
with bloody hands and f-4 forms.
Are we more than halfway, mom?

How many how many women
travel with a couple of children?
and no man.
They are young women,
strong and delicate, plump, some of them beautiful.
That's why we have bridges,
David, so we can cross rivers.
No, we aren't halfway yet, honey.

The children are desirous, contented.

Intellectual, sexual beings, the women
have needs that draw them

a long way, across rivers:
social, moral, foolish, patient travailers.

Mount Olympus towers across the Sound
cloudheaded in evening.

She only cried for a moment.

The House of the Spider:
A Spell to Weave

He rides by, the rider,
the hunter,
the cunter.
Grandmother, hide her.

He rides past, the master,
has passed her,
has lost her.
Hang quiet, spider.

Good riddance the rider!
The spinster,
the sister,
live here beside her.

They are together,
the brother,
no other.
Here at the center.

For June Jordan

Called after summer and the deep river,
there among us cool
and shallow others,
when I said *we are all kings,* you
shook your fierce kingly head, denying.
No kings any more! you said.
I keep seeing what you were saying
and that you led
clear free of rule
to our own where,
across the river in the summer,
that far shore,
nobody ever, nobody ever
singing of war.

At the Party

The women over fifty
are convex from collarbone to crotch,
scarred armor nobly curved.
Their eyes look out from lines
through you, like the eyes of lions.
Unexpectant, unforgiving, calm,
they can eat children.
They eat celery and make smalltalk.
Sometimes when they touch each other's arms
they weep for a moment.

Old Bag

Officer officer
I lost my bag

Put it down somewhere lady?

no no
they took it

Got a description?

they were nice young men
I think
but they didn't
but when I
they'd already thrown it away

What was in it?

Trouble.
It was just an old one
catch wouldn't even fasten
no good any more but when I was rich
you know
think what was in it

Lady are you reporting something stolen?

no I can't seem to tell you
why I want to tell you
about my children

The Woman with the Shopping Cart
Who Sleeps in Doorways

Shawled in plastic,
you push on past,
grey eyes staring
under grey hair.

I know how to
just look through you
like cold water
running through air.

But you rise up
in my mind's eye
at home, later.
I see you clear.

And what I own,
you've got it in
your shopping cart.
Look at it there.

His Daughter

His daughter,
the visionary warrior, the silent man
of whom there is no photograph,
the true fragile hero
who lost what he won as he won it
through massacre to sacrifice,
this man, Crazy Horse, his daughter,
what became of her?
        She died a child.
        After that there were no victories.
What was her name, that child?
        Her father named her.
        He gave her this name:
        They Will Fear Her.

The Menstrual Lodge

Accepting the heavy destiny of power,
I went to the small house when the time came.
I ate no meat, looked no one in the eye,
and scratched my fleabites with a stick:
to touch myself would close the circle
that must be open so a man can enter.
After five days I came home,
having washed myself and all I touched and wore
in Bear Creek, washed away the sign,
the color, and the smell of power.

It was no use. Nothing,
no ritual or servitude or shame,
unmade my power, or your fear.

You waited in the thickets in the winter rain
as I went alone from the small house.
You beat my head and face and raped me
and went to boast. When my womb swelled,
your friends made a small circle with you:
            We all fucked that one.
            Who knows who's the father?

By Bear Creek I gave birth, in Bear Creek
I drowned it. Who knows who's the mother?
Its father was your fear of me.

I am the dirt beneath your feet.
What are you frightened of? Go fight your wars,
be great in club and lodge and politics.
When you find out what power is, come back.

I am the dirt, and the raincloud, and the rain.
The walls of my house are the steps I walk
from day of birth around the work I work,
from giving birth to day of death.
The roof of my house is thunder,
the doorway is the wind.
I keep this house, this great house.

When will you come in?

Hunger

Full of age and tears,
full of years and rage,
and empty of all but heartache, need
to speak, craving, yearning
to learn the saving
word:
the word,
the first
word:
            MA
                        cow moo, sheep bleat,
round sound, open, whole,
all soft, valley word,
word of the waters,
not over not above
but under, on, in, the tongue of the daughters,
of the lovers, the many,
the any, the tender language hanging
like catkins, falling like rain,
rising like mushrooms and thunder,
answering hunger,
I'll speak brokenly and hear
spoken and sweetly sung
my dear native tongue.
I'll give food and be fed.
I'll eat our words like bread.

PART THREE: WORDS

PART THREE WORDS

Wild Oats and Fireweed

I dream of you,
I dream of you jumping,
Rabbit, jackrabbit, and quail.

A foolish daughter of immigrants,
prodigal, hybrid,
I was promiscuous.

The weed beside the road
casts its seed wide.

It furthers to cross the great water.

Old, I am only
this dirt, returning
to this ground,
a sharecropper.
O my America! my new-found-land!

The wild oats,
even, are foreign.

Weed and worthless foolsgold of the hills
of my childhood, my California,
let me be worthy
the stone: the pollen:
the word spoken where the water rises:
the four colors of earth.
Let me in life hold

and pass before dying
the pouch of the silent things
of the six directions.
Let me dream,
let me dream of you jumping,
rabbit, jackrabbit, and quail.

The red weed by roadsides
flowers, in clearcuts and burns
and the wastes of St Helens,
a tall, feathered dancer,
casting its ash-seeds.

O my America!
From the north ice, the raven's,
through the coyote-colored lands
and the Sun's heights and empires
to the south ice, the fireland,
they stand, the Rockies, Andes, vertebrae,
backbone of the black vulture
nailed to the barnside,
the vermin, the varmint.

My body is nail
and condor.
My breath is bullet
and feather.

I return, I turn, I turn in place.
I am my inheritance.

On the edge of the mountain a cloud hangs
and my heart
my heart
my heart hangs with it.

Late I have learned the last direction.
May I before death
learn some words of my language.

The Organ

Inside my ribcage
is a black gland,
inert, dull-surfaced.
It absorbs words.
Nothing comes out.
From it long processes,
dendrites, extend
to certain graves
and ideas.
                    Signals
come to it, seldom, obscure.
It transmits them
to nerve and mind
as pure fear.
                    That is its function,
perhaps. All that is certain:
without it
the heart stops.

For Bill Stafford

I will thank William
the willing giver.
"When you can't write?"—
"I lower my standards,"
he said, with the sweetest smile.
We saw the banners bowing
to earth with the gesture
of grasses, of willows, of water,
of all that will go lower.
Under them armies are buried.

For Helene Cixous

"Je suis là où ça parle"

I'm there where
it's talking
Where that speaks I
am in that talking place
                  Where
that says
my being is
        Where
my being there
is speaking
I am
    and so
laughing
in a stone ear

To Gary and Allen and All with Love

I know you know about Coyote,
but not sure you noticed
when she ate your dhoti.

Boys, there's been an operation.
Good old poets. Us girls done had phallus
up to here. Things coming round now.

Hey little all head and tail,
meet Ms Egg! One at a time now,
but quick, the bitch'll fool you.

She is a trickster. Listen, fellows,
I'm only your old kid sister,
hey wait, hey please turn round?

What cubs suck these yellow tits?
If you don't who'll tell us? In what words?
It ain't Om I don't think.
No padre humming here I guess.

Wild milk, it's sweet,
but this lullaby sears beards.
God, what a stink here! Yes, child. Yes.

Come help us, semblables, brother hypocrites,
littersibs, old slobs, come bring your turds,
help us help mama to unbuild.

Silence

I had a little naked thought
slipped out between my thighs
and ran before it could be caught
and flew without having been taught,
O see how quick it flies!
My baby thought, my little bird
all rosy naked goes.
I must sew word to word to word
and button up its clothes
and so it grows and walks and talks and dies.
When I am dead look for the rose
that grows between my eyes.
Birds will perch on leaf and thorn,
silent birds to silence born.

A Private Ceremony of Public Mourning for the Language of the People Called Wappo

> The Wappo go under an unaboriginal name which is too well established to make its replacement possible. It is an Americanization of Spanish Guapo, "brave," a sobriquet which they earned in Mission times by their stubborn resistance to the military adjuncts of the Franciscan establishments.
>
> —A. L. Kroeber, *Handbook of the Indians of California*, 1919

> The young women began their frightful dance, which consists of two leaps on each foot alternately, causing the body to rock to-and-fro; and either hand was thrust out with the swaying . . . while the breath was forced out with violence between the teeth, in regular cadence, with a harsh and grunting sound of *heh!* . . . We were beholding now, at last, the great dance for the dead.
>
> —Stephen Powers, *Tribes of California*, 1877

There are none
there are not   none   no
none left to live not one
no tongue not one that knows
one word not one
and no name no: what
was their name?
That people?
Called by those that killed them Brave.
Died, and their names died.
Nameless go on nameless knolls like dead of animals.
Tongue word and language and all sweet
discourse of reason and of love
beneath the leafy roof
silent all gone silent as the grave

lost   gone   and there are none
not   one.

It is the end of August:
dancing time.
Young women jump
twice on the left foot
twice on the right foot
twice on the left foot
twice on the right foot
twice on the left foot
twice on the right foot
twice on the left foot
twice on the right foot
rocking the body and the hands thrust
out and the breath forced
out between the teeth *heh*
hours *heh* all *heh* night *heh* dance *heh*
dance for all the dead who died
this year or in this valley of the hills
whose names we do not know.

O women of my people!
Dance for the forgotten
on the left foot twice
on the right foot twice
stamping and rocking and crying
the dance we have forgotten,
the old dance of the women.
Dance on our grave their dance,
all night, all night, all night, all night.

PART FOUR: WOMEN

The Song of the Torus

I am a torus.
No bull no no
but torus with an O,
beloved of the topologist
of me beloved moren 30 year agone
       but not reciprocal no no.
       A hollow lad he was
but I am hollower
having had the very womb excised and being void
in the middle, not the heart or heart of hearts, but there,
where you came from, darling,
reader dear. Including me.
       Reciprocal.
Torus am I, the shape that holds no thing.
I'm Men-an-Tol, the wedding ring.
I am the bear that cannot bear no more.

In the empty space
do you perceive a star?
Does Reason twinkle steadfast there
above dry sedges of the Baby Lake
(where once the child of the topologist
fluttered a month and did not come to be
not to the age of Reason no not to any age)?
What shines through my nothing?
I can see the shadow that it casts.
Tell me, tell me, you who look right through me,
wise doctors!

I have borne, I have borne, I have borne.
What next, I wonder?

I'm not unmothered yet;
although I brought her ashes home upon my lap,
and took the knife and cut the bleeding part away,
yet the old woman will not sleep.
She mates with bears and stars to find
what may a wombless woman bring to term
and suckle with the mind's sweet milk
and rock, and sing to, sing the lullaby.

The Present

That girl saw
a white fawn come
beside a dun doe
to her
on a high turn
before the sun.

She sees
them stand and gaze
with eyes that do not name.
She held out her hand.
Slow,
they turn and go,
but the white
fawn looks back.

I have tried to understand.
White does not mean.
I look back

and she is in
the light before the sun
and a doe
and her white fawn come.

For Katya

You know, love
you know, love
you aren't the only one that ever

They always shut us up in towers
ever since once upon a

So we learn alone there
arts of unlocking

Till the old terrors
shed wolfskin and stand brothers

by the alder lake at the edge of April

and the waiting's over

T.C.K.B.K.Q.,
Telluride 1897—Berkeley 1979

I try to get my mother back.
With difficulty. I have to scold her—
Why did you do that?
Why were you like that?
     Fragments. Glances.
The delicate halfmoon of the nail.
There! for a moment I hold her—
     a woman of forty
     writing the monthly payments.
     Wearing the silver seven-turquoise ring
     from the middle of the world,
     at a high desk by a glass door
     to a balcony under redwoods,
     she keeps the books of the household.
The accounts are paid,
and the ring she gave me
at the roots of the redwoods.

If I don't scold but coax her—
     Come on, come down, you beauty
     in highlaced boots,
     girl riding or long-striding
     through a mining town in the Rockies,
come, come before me,
before you can love or fear me!

But the brothers and shadowy father
cling to her. She was many,
she always comes bringing the others,

the husbands, the sons, myself.
I don't want them. I want her,
whom her lovers encircled, concealed
with the unending bridal,
her in the seventh of the seven ways,
the woman inside the women.
Not hearth-warmth, bed-warmth, breast-warmth,
but the mortal light
revealed.

If I begin to let go
will I glimpse one moment
the shining deep there
in earth, the unmined silver,
or high, far, oh, above her birth
before the daylight, snow
on those peaks where a river starts
in a long glimmering falling through dark air?

While the Old Men Make Ready to Kill

Eternal Life sits on the leaf
cleaning green wings with tiny legs.
Eternal Life, a four-horned turd,
winds graceful up the hemlock stalk.
Eternal Life with garnet facet eyes
alights and realights from blade to blade
of the Eternal Life that grows from every root.
　　　And still we rant of heaven
and breathe it in and still spit poison out.
The snake is innocent and wise: we spurn
Eternal Life beneath our heel.
I pray you, grass, return, erase.
I pray you, slug and worm,
you who eat hemlock, can you stomach us?
I pray you, air, forgive us.
I pray you, life, forget—
　　　　　　　　　　Stop.
There is a finger on my lips
no longer than a beetle's leg.
A little worm is in my daughter's womb
who innocent and wise
stops me and will not let me prophesy.
　　　For Cassandra must be virgin
(as all women are, this much I've lived to learn)
but in man's definition; she must speak
to men in the language of men with a man's tongue,
and then they will not hear her,
because they understand her.
But I talk now in the thick tongue of a woman
to an unborn baby.
In that language is no prophecy.

Twice I bore death, thrice I bore life,
I know this language well.
I know how you learn it.
    Baby, baby, maybe to be born,
little one, fear nothing.
You can hear me, child.
Sleep and be born,
the morning will come.
The grass grows green, the small flies sing,
welcome here and never fear.
You are the Life Eternal,
baby, baby, maybe to be born.
Sweet summer's daughter's child of winter,
come to her, come to me, come.

The Photograph of Lyra Sofia

You look out from that ancient Emma Goldman face
two hours old
with little slitty eyes still seeing uterus
and lips sticky with colostrum
not even knowing what milk is yet,
and a will of iron.
You look like your daddy
and my Great Aunt Betsy
and Red Emma and that one
who comes of her own will and in due time
out to the sunny places
to play a while that she is not queen
below in realms of iron and the night.
O Revolutionary! turn
to her whose hands hold leaves
and spiky grasses, who sings the birds,
sower, sorrower, giver, griever.
Be gentle with your mother, learn
with her the will of water.

Lyra, 26 November 85

Twelve-moon girl!
One day past full
into the dark falling,
rises, brightens,
dims, brightens,
over clouds
in mists
very high
up, ball-bubble
shining rising,
soft, round,
standing up, falling over,
laughing,
this girl's moon.
This small girl's
twelfth moon
shining.

For the New House

May this house be full of kitchen smells
and shadows and toys and nests of mice
and roars of rage and waterfalls of tears
and deep sexual silences and sounds
of mysterious origin never explained
and troves and keepsakes and a lot of junk
and a flowing like a warm wind only slower
blowing the leaves of trees and books and the fish-years
of a child's life silvery flickering
quick, quick in the slow incessant gust
that billows out the curtains a moment
all those years from now, ago.
May the sills and doorframes
be in blessing blest at every passing.
May the roof but not the rooms know rain.
May the windows know clearly
the branch and flower of the apple tree.
And may you be in this house
as the music is in the instrument.

Ella Peavy's Birthday

Beautiful exotic insects,
the grandchildren fly in and out
from New York and Bloomington.
Aunt Trella felt a little faint
before dinner, but eats her gentle way
through seconds of marshmallow fruit salad.
Radiant today and eighty-five,
Peavy puts on the plastic piggy-snout
and grunts contentedly
above bright wrapping-paper ruins,
while tiny great-grandchildren fizz and bounce
in the fountain of everybody laughing.

The Old Falling Down

In the old falling-down
house of my childhood
I go down-
stairs to sleep out-
side on the porch
under stars and dream
of trying to go up-
stairs but there are no
stairs so I climb
hand over hand clambering
scared and when I get there
to my high room, find
no bed, no chair, bare floor.

The Light

The light is eating me
and has eaten my Peruvian   letter by letter,
as it ate the horses   word by word.
of my childhood.
It has eaten   By answering strangers,
the spare parts of my soul   by displacing anger,
and the planetshadows
I used to hide in.   and by good works
I feed the sharks.

It has eaten bone
and opal.   Not faith and not good works
but good work only
It is eating syntax.   casts a shadow.
It has left me only   How shall I do that?—
an old woman talking
in a dark house.

Tenses

I am an old mad woman beating with a spoon
for madness of a whining saw
on a summer afternoon.
An old mad angry impotence:
Stop that! Stop that!
And beat and beat the spoon upon the table.
A bad baby, an animal gone wrong.

What's Mind? Its continuity.

There was a time before this noise that drives me mad.
There will be silence after. There will be.

Terrible the cage of the present tense
and unavailing rage
and interminable pain:
without foresight or memory
the old mad monkey beats and beats the spoon.
No promise kept, nothing left
but the whining saw that occupies the brain.

Inventory

The map of the tributaries of the Amazon
in blue, on the right thigh;
lesser riversystems
on the lower left leg.
Extremities
far more extreme:
knobbed, wired, bent, and multiknuckled.
Some dun cloud
drifts across the color of the eye,
that aged nestling in its baggy nest,
still avid, still insatiable.
Replacement of cheek by jowl,
of curve by hook or crook.
Moles, warts, wenlets, cancerlings,
a distressed finish, constellations,
here the Twins,
there the Cluster, fleshy Pleiades
coming out thick at evening of the skin—
pied beauty—there is none
that hath not some Strangeness
in the Proportion.
So the columnar what was waist
sockets to the cushioned pediment
of hips and buttocks. Parts are missing. Scars
lie smiling soft and small among the folds
and hillocks of that broad countryside.
O have I not my rivers and my stars,
my wrinkled ranges in the Western sun?
O have I not my Strangeness?
I am this continent,

and still explore and find no boundary,
for the far sandy beaches of my mind
where soft vast waves and winds erase
the words, the faces—this is still
endless, this is endless still.
I am that wind, that ocean.

Silk Days

Boat-prow poking close to the
buttons, or wide scythe sweeps
across the back acres, or
cat-nosing up into a pleat:
it reminds me. I like
getting it
right, smooth,
the sleeves keen-creased.

Ironing smells like ironing.
It isn't really like
anything. Doesn't need
a simile.
Has its own equipment.

My great-aunt taught me:
sprinkler-bottle, rolled up half an hour,
wetfinger hiss-test,
hem-nudging, care on the collar.
In ten minutes, on a mangle,
she could do a dress shirt.
It can be an art.

It used to be hard work,
no time, all cotton, all the kids.
These days I go in silk,

Empress of China, wash and iron
when I choose to,
pleasuring, getting it
right, a good job,
easy going,
smooth as silk.

A Meditation on a Marriage

From my California, my great land
of gold and complications, wilderness,
enormous cities built on faults,
austere, bizarre, and inexhaustible
vineyards, valleys crowded with visions,

to your Georgia of red dirt
farms, where trees are all one green,
a bony piny sandy silence,
your Georgia of slow rivers, graves,
islands, that quiet place,

how could I come with all my California?

I see them come with open hands,
transparent, sharing everything,
giving and cleaving, nothing kept,
the emigrants that leave their motherland
for love and never look behind.

But if I would how could I give you
California? and I have to live
there, working the creeks my veins, the mines.
Or you could you leave Georgia,
leaving your bones behind,
and give me more than silence?

So we have made these no-one's-lands
by meeting where we never know
when we shall meet or not,
like spies or pioneers

telling the news in low voices
down in the willow coulees
in a grey evening, inland.

We met at sea,
married in a foreign language:
what wonder
if we cross a continent on foot
each time to find each other
at secret borders
bringing
of all my streams and darknesses of gold
and your deep graves and islands
a feather
a flake of mica
a willow leaf
that is our country,
ours alone.

Spell

An unknotting.
A disbraidment.
  A great magic—
What is magic?

I release me.